A Wolf's Da

"He huffed and he puffed and my house fell down like a leaf in the wind. I was homeless in a flash!" Paul Pig belted, tossing his straw hat in the air.

"He blew down my house and my brother's, too. He even tried to blow down my sister's house."

Judge Olivia turned toward Walter, motioning with her wing. "Walter, is that what happened that day?"

FAIRY TALE VERSUS

THE 3 PIGS VS. THE WOLF

WRITTEN BY
TIFFANY OBENG

ILLUSTRATED BY
SURYA GUNAWAN

SUGAR COOKIE BOOKS™

Copyright © 2024 by Tiffany Obeng
Cover art and interior illustrations © 2024 by Tiffany Obeng
Fairy Tale Versus ™ series created by Tiffany Obeng

All rights reserved. No part of this book may be reproduced, transmitted, or stored in an information retrieval system in any form or by any means, graphic, electronic, or mechanical, including photocopying, taping, and recording, i9ncluding YouTube, without prior written permission from the publisher. Contact sugarcookiebooks@gmail.com for all inquiries.

Visit us on the Web!
Sugarcookiebooks.com

Educators and librarians, for a variety of teaching tools, visit us at www.teacherspayteachers.com/store/sugar-cookie-books

Library of Congress Cataloguing in Publication Data available upon request.
LCCN 2024918879
ISBN 978-1-959075-24-0

Published in the United States by Sugar Cookie Books, an imprint.

For all future lawyers, judges, and seekers of justice and fairness.

-Tiffany Obeng

Chapter 1

Once upon a time in the heart of Woodland Forest, lived a little owl named Olivia Otomayor. Olivia had big amber eyes and an even bigger pair of glasses that she wore high on her beak. Even as an owlet, Olivia always loved reading.

Her tree house bedroom was stuffed to the branches with books of all sorts. Her favorite books were law books that filled every shelf and corner. Olivia kept notepads nearby, so she could easily scribble notes about the different forest laws. On her bedroom wall hung a poster of her hero, Hamala Karris, the famous lawyer who believed justice was for everyone!

All the forest animals thought Olivia was smart, kind, and fair. They always went to Olivia to help them with their problems. So, not too long ago, the forest community selected Olivia for the important role of Judge of the Woodland Forest Court. Now, Olivia would be able to help her friends using the laws that she loved learning.

Even though Olivia was so excited to be the new judge, she was also a little nervous. She often wondered, *What if she made a mistake? What if her decision made one of her friends sad?*

One bright morning, there was a sudden rap on the door of Olivia's hollow tree home. It was her best friend, William, a lively woodpecker with bright red feathers on his head and black and white feathers on his body. He often wore a small bow tie to show he was ready for business.

William knew everything going on in the forest. He was always right by Olivia's side when she helped the forest community with their problems. He had encouraged Olivia to accept the honorable job as the forest judge. Of course, he worked as the court bailiff perched right beside Olivia, keeping order in the court.

"Your Honor, we have a big problem that needs your help right away," William chirped. "It's the three pigs and the wolf!"

Olivia felt a flutter of nerves in her stomach. She was still getting used to being called, "Your Honor." She smoothed down her soft brown feathers and asked, "What happened?"

"They say Walter destroyed Paul's straw house and Patrick's stick house with his mighty breath," William explained.

"And what about Penelope's brick house?"

William shrugged his feathery shoulders. "He tried to blow it down, but it was too strong for him."

Olivia adjusted her glasses, as she always did when she was nervous. "Alright, I guess we should get to the courthouse right away?" Olivia said more as a question than a statement.

Sensing Olivia's uncertainty, William placed a wing on his friend's shoulder. "Olivia, this might be your first case as Judge, but you have always tried your hardest to make the forest a fair and happy place for us all. This time will be no different."

Olivia slowly lifted her head and started a smile. "I guess you're right, William. Let's not keep our friends waiting, huh?"

With that, Olivia and William headed to the Woodland Forest Court.

Chapter 2

The Woodland Forest Court was nestled in the middle-most part of the forest. A weathered wooden sign hung above its entrance door. "Woodland Forest Court" was carved on it. The courthouse was surrounded by tall redwoods and fragrant pine trees that always bore leaves the color of fall. Their branches swayed gently in the breeze, providing a soothing backdrop to the serious business that would be conducted inside. A dirt path lined with colorful wildflowers and mushroom circles led up to the three courthouse steps.

As Olivia and William arrived at the busy courthouse, Olivia could feel her nerves in her throat. Olivia entered the courthouse's sturdy oakwood walls and beelined it to the Judge's Chambers. Olivia's heart raced as she slipped on her black judge's robe that was two, maybe three, sizes too big. She faced the mirror, giving herself a once over. She adjusted her glasses and took a few deep breaths. Then, Olivia emerged from her chambers, landing on her perch behind the large wooden bench.

"Order in the court!" William squawked, tapping his beak against the Judge's Bench. "We are here today to hear the case of the Three Pigs versus the Wolf." The bustling courtroom fell instantly silent.

On one side of the courtroom sat the three pigs - Paul in his simple straw hat and oversized overalls, Patrick in his stylish jacket and pants, and Penelope in a pink dress and hair bow.

On the other side of the courtroom sat the wolf. Walter was big and gray with sharp ears and bright yellow eyes. He wore jeans and a black jacket over his clean fur. He sat next to his lawyer; a scruffy coyote named Carl. Carl's outfit of choice - a raggedy suit jacket, a too big necktie, and a too tight hat – did not hide his tan and brown fur that looked as if it had not been brushed in a while.

William beckoned, "Paul Pig, please begin by telling us why you are suing the wolf."

Paul, the oldest of the three pig siblings, stood on wobbly legs. "Your Honor, we're here today because the Wolf blew down my home and I'll prove he did it on purpose!"

The pig's accusation riled Walter. He banged his paw on the table and growled, "I'm not guilty, you bacon bits!" His sharp ears straightened. His bright yellow eyes glowed.

Thunderous snorts and angry oinks from the pigs' family echoed off the oakwood walls. William flapped his wings to calm them down and regain order.

When the room was quiet again, Olivia warned Walter, "This is a courtroom, not a, uh, jungle. Another outburst and you will be in…in…in big trouble, Walter." She hoped her stutter and stammer had not betrayed her serious threat.

Walter gulped and recoiled in his seat. His sharp ears dulled and his yellow eyes dimmed. Olivia sat up a little straighter, feeling a bit surer of herself after standing up to the wolf. She turned her attention back to Paul,

nodding for him to continue.

"Yes, Your Honor. As I was saying, I had just finished building my house, feeling proud, when suddenly, the Wolf appeared at my door!" Paul turned toward Walter pointing his hoof.

"He huffed and he puffed and my house fell down like a leaf in the wind. I was homeless in a flash!" Paul belted, tossing his straw hat in the air.

"He blew down my house and my brother's, too. He even tried to blow down my sister's house."

Olivia felt sorry for Paul and the pig family. She knew the whole ordeal must have been terrifying for them. And now they were homeless.

Olivia shook her head in an effort to refocus on the trial. She could not let her feelings get in the way of being fair. She needed to keep an open mind and listen to both sides before reaching any conclusions. She motioned with her wing. "And how do you respond, Walter?"

Chapter 3

Speaking for Walter, Carl began, "Your Honor, we will prove that my client was just following his instincts as a predator of the forest. You see, the three pigs *chose* to build their homes right where wolves like Walter roam. To a hungry wolf, those straw and stick houses were like wrapping paper on a yummy snack. Walter couldn't help himself —"

Olivia interrupted, "Mr. Coyote, all of us forest creatures must coexist with each other and that includes wolves."

"Yes, well, even so, we will prove that Walter did not *mean* to destroy Paul and Patrick's weak homes. It was just an

accident from sneezing too hard! Who can control the force of their sneezes?" Carl asked, turning toward the audience.

"It would not have been long before their homes would have fallen from the effects of nature anyway. My client just quickened the inevitable...accidentally."

The pigs' family snorted at the coyote as he returned to his seat beside the wolf. Olivia's brow furrowed as she thought about what Carl said. Paul and Patrick's houses had fallen down easily and Penelope's brick house had stood strong. Both Paul and Carl had made good points. She realized this case was different from the simple forest disputes. This was definitely not going to be an easy or quick decision. Olivia took a long, deep breath and then banged her gavel.

"That's enough for today," she announced. "Let's get some rest and start again tomorrow morning."

After everyone had left, William flew over to Olivia. "I know today was tense, but you will figure out this mess between the pigs and the wolf. You always do."

"Yes, I know you're right," she thanked

William for the vote of confidence. But on the inside, Olivia wondered if she really could make sense of it all this time.

That night, Olivia stayed up late re-reading her law books on property damage and bad intentions. When she'd finished, Olivia looked out at the forest and gazed at the twinkling stars. Tomorrow was going to be a showdown, and now, she was ready to face it.

"Tomorrow, justice will be served," she whispered to the moon.

Chapter 4

All of the forest was talking about the big case between the three pigs and the wolf. So it was no surprise that the next morning, forest animals were lined up early to get good seats in the courtroom. The squirrels tried to find the best spots to peer inside, and field mice played cheerful music to keep everyone in a good mood.

Inside the courthouse, Patrick and Penelope were getting ready for their big moment. Today, they were taking the witness stand to help prove their brother's case that Walter had blown down their homes on purpose. Patrick and Penelope went over their stories one more time. Their determination was greater than their nerves.

"We have to be really clear today," Paul said, looking from one sibling to the other. "The wolf's lawyer is going to try

to find problems with what we say and we can't let him."

Patrick nodded, his curly tail spinning around. "After I tell everyone how the wolf blew down my stick house, he won't get away with this. They'll know he did it all on purpose."

Just then, William appeared at the courtroom doorway, waving them inside. "It's time! Judge Otomayor is ready to resume the trial!"

As forest creatures hurried past them, Penelope looked at Paul seriously. "This is our chance to make things right,

Big Brother."

Paul put his hoof on her shoulder. "You'll do great on the stand, Sis. We're counting on you."

The three pigs walked into the courtroom. The courtroom crowd cheered them on. The crowd "booed" when the wolf and his lawyer came in.

"Quiet! We need order in the court!" William squawked and rapped his beak on the bench. Olivia also hammered her gavel two times. The courtroom chatter stopped abruptly. Olivia focused on the pigs and the wolf.

"Very well, let's pick up where we left off yesterday. Paul, you may call your first witness to the stand."

Chapter 5

Patrick was the youngest brother and owner of the destroyed stick home. He told everyone about the day Walter Wolf came and blew his house down with his mighty breath.

"I am a little pig with limited means. I could only afford to build a modest stick house. I worked really hard on my stick house. I searched the forest for strong sticks and I wove them together very carefully. But by the hair of my chinny-chin-chin, the wolf blew it all down! On purpose! It was quite scary!" Sweat drops flew from Patrick's forehead.

Paul piped up, "Your Honor, my brother would like to show you the pieces of his stick house as proof of the damage the wolf caused to his home."

"Ah, yes, that's right." Patrick picked up a sack, walked over to Olivia, and began pouring broken sticks onto Olivia's bench.

But Carl objected, "How do we know *those* sticks are from Patrick's house? There are broken sticks *everywhere* in the forest."

Olivia agreed, "That's a good point, Mr. Coyote. Patrick, if you cannot prove

these sticks are really from your house, you will have to put them away."

Patrick's pink cheeks flushed red as he quickly put the sticks back into the sack. He held the sack tight against his chest and scampered back to his seat on the witness stand. For a moment, he wished he could hide in the sack until the trial was over.

After a few seconds, Patrick finished, "I would have been a rump roast under the pile of rubble if it had not been for my big brother, Paul, saving me." He placed his hooves over his heart and looked at his brother adoringly.

The courtroom crowd murmured soft sounds of condolences. But, unmoved, Carl taunted Patrick, "Are stick houses even strong enough to keep you safe?"

Patrick stuttered, "Y-y-yes, stick houses, and straw houses for that matter, are quite suitable for forest living. Us forest animals have built abodes out of these common materials for ages."

"Is that so?" Carl quipped.

"It is so," replied a voice not belonging to Patrick.

Chapter 6

All eyes were on Penelope as she took the witness stand. She was an expert in building things. She knew all about building materials, structural strength, and wind resistance. Paul was counting on her to prove their case against the wolf.

"Your Honor, forest friends," she began, "I'm here to share what I know about my brothers' homes."

She pulled out a blueprint with a picture of a straw house and a stick house drawn on it.

"It's true. We have used straw and sticks to build our forest homes for years. But neither straw nor stick is the best building material for a sustainable dwelling."

Everyone leaned forward curious. The pig brothers exchanged worried glances. Even Olivia adjusted her glasses. *This was not looking too good for the pig siblings*, she thought.

"Clay bricks like the ones I used for

my house are the best for shelter and lasting security. They can withstand forest elements, strong winds...and the Wolf's huffs," she said, cutting her eyes at Walter. The room was so silent, you could hear a pine needle drop.

Carl cleared his throat and stood with his fists pressed firmly on the table. "Judge Otomayor, you must dismiss the charges against Walter. By Penelope's own 'expert' words," Carl gestured with air quotes, "Walter's just not responsible for the damage to the pigs' homes. Sticks and straw are not strong enough to withstand, well, anything. Their houses were simply not durable and that's not Walter's fault. Case closed." Carl did an exaggerated shoulder shrug before sitting back down.

Paul squealed, "But Your Honor, my brother and I did our best with what we had. Should we get in trouble just because we didn't use bricks?"

"And should my client be punished for blowing his breath?" Carl argued back.

Olivia raised her wing, signaling for everyone to calm down. Olivia's feathers ruffled under her robe. She wondered, *Had the coyote found a big problem in the case after all.* She needed to hear more before making her decision. She motioned for Penelope to continue.

"Thank you, Your Honor." Penelope looked over the courtroom audience, making sure she had everyone's undivided attention before continuing.

"But the *way* Paul's house fell, needed *more* than just forest winds and typical forest weather. You see, stick and straw homes, *especially* ones that are new and well-built like my brothers', need *a lot* of direct force and pressure to fall down. Direct force and pressure just like the intentional huffing and puffing by the Big Bad Wolf!"

As Penelope stepped down from the witness stand, the courtroom buzzed with amusement. Olivia glanced over at the wolf. He twiddled his paw thumbs and his eyes darted from side to side, competing with Carl's fast scribbling on his notepad. Olivia wondered what Walter would say to try to prove his innocence.

Chapter 7

It was finally Walter's turn to tell his side of the story. Carl called Walter to the witness stand. Walter walked to the front of the courtroom, meeting the eyes of the animals watching him. When he reached the stand, he looked at Olivia. Her big amber eyes only stared back at him.

Walter turned to address the courtroom. "On that fateful day, I was really hungry. I had been on a strict liquid protein diet." Even Walter had to admit that a wolf on a liquid diet was quite unusual.

"When I smelled something delicious coming from the pigs' houses, I couldn't help but follow my nose. The blazing hot sun and their sweat from building their homes created a sweet, tasty aroma of pork that I could not ignore." Walter's mouth watered at the memory.

"I knocked on each door politely,

hoping they would be good forest citizens. But the pigs were downright rude to me.

"They teased me with their chant, '*Not by the hair of my chinny-chin-chin.*' They didn't offer me any food, not even a snack. They hurt my feelings." Walter lowered his yellow eyes as his voice trailed off.

Paul jumped to his hooves, "You cannot go around destroying our homes because you're hurt or mad, Walter!"

"But that's just it. I was not trying to blow down your homes. I was actually coming down with a bad case of sneezes that day. I sneeze when I'm starved, you see?" Walter pulled a doctor's note from his jacket pocket and handed it to Olivia.

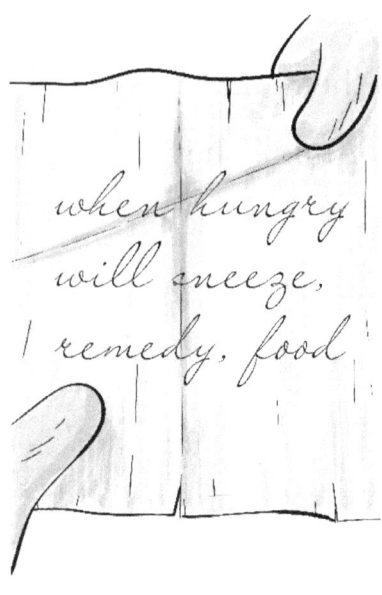

"And those houses were just weak tinderboxes. They were frail and easily toppled. It wasn't my fault they fell down," He pleaded. Nervous chuckles arose in the courtroom.

"I honestly didn't know they would fall down! How could I? I'm a hungry wolf, not a building expert." Walter pointed toward Penelope who smoothed her pink dress.

"I hear what you all call me: The Big Bad Wolf. You fear me and you reject me and you don't even know me. Yes, I am bound by my instincts and driven by my nature, but I'm also a member of this forest community just like each and every one of you. You cannot change who you are and neither can I. Nor do I wish to."

As Walter returned to his seat, the courtroom filled with thoughtful whispers. Olivia narrowed her eyes in deep thought. The wolf's testimony had given them all something to ponder.

Chapter 8

Paul Pig and the lawyer, Carl Coyote, had one final chance to convince the court whether Walter had destroyed the pigs' homes on purpose or not.

Paul spoke first. "Your Honor and friends of the court, I stand before you today as a victim of unjust destruction.

Even if my house was made of straw, and my brother's house of sticks, does that mean it's okay for the wolf to destroy them? Shouldn't we all feel safe and happy in our homes, no matter what they're made of? We ask the court to hold the wolf responsible for his actions."

Paul returned to his seat. His brother and sister nodded their heads and clapped their hooves in support.

Next, Carl spoke, "And I ask the court to give my client a fair chance. Walter is not the Big Bad Wolf that everyone makes him out to be. He's just a hungry wolf who had a hunger-induced sneeze attack that happened to knock down the pigs' weak stacks of straw and sticks. The pig brothers could have avoided this fate by helping Walter to a snack or by building better homes. They chose to do neither. So, I ask you: Is Walter really responsible for the pigs' poor choices?"

As Carl sat back down, Walter gave him a grateful nod, hoping his words had made a difference.

Now it was time for Olivia to make her decision. Olivia felt flutters in her tummy again. *What if she got it wrong?* She dreaded the thought of disappointing whichever party ended up losing the case.

Olivia looked over her notes and the evidence carefully. She knew that being fair and paying attention to every detail was the way to find the truth. She looked out of the window at the forest trees swaying gently in the forest wind. She inhaled deeply and exhaled slowly. The courtroom was thick with suspense as they waited to hear Olivia's decision.

Finally, Olivia adjusted her glasses and announced the verdict. "After care-

fully considering all the evidence and arguments, I've decided that there is *not* enough evidence to prove that Walter blew down the pig brothers' homes on purpose."

The entire courtroom crowd gasped. Walter's and Carl's jaws dropped wide. They leaned forward in their seats hopeful. The pig siblings hugged each other tight.

"But," Olivia said firmly, "there *is* enough evidence to prove Walter did in deed destroy Paul's straw house and Patrick's stick house even if he did so accidentally."

The pigs erupted in oinks of cheer! William rapped his beak and Olivia banged her gavel.

Olivia finished, "Instead of punishment, I have come up with a fair resolution. Walter, you must help Paul and Patrick rebuild their homes. And Walter, you must learn to control your big breaths. Court adjourned." Olivia banged her gavel a final time.

Walter sat back in his chair feeling slightly defeated, but grateful for the fair ruling overall. The three pigs were a little disappointed, but ultimately trusted Olivia's judgment as well.

As the courtroom emptied, William hopped over to Olivia and placed a wing on her shoulder. "Well, you did it, Olivia. Just like we knew you would. I'd say your first official case was a grand success."

Olivia allowed herself a small smile that grew into a wide smile. "You're right, William. I did do it!"

Over the next few weeks, Paul, Patrick and Walter worked together to rebuild their homes. Forest friends freely gave bricks and other building materials, and Penelope oversaw the building process.

As they worked together, the pigs learned Walter was not so "big and bad." All of the forest animals realized kindness and understanding was the key to living together happily and became unexpected friends. And so, Woodland Forest became a happier place for all forest creatures and everyone lived **happily ever after**.

Discussion Questions

1. Olivia was known among her forest friends for being smart and fair. How do your friends describe you?
2. Olivia doubts herself when she makes big decisions. How did Olivia overcome her doubts and become more confident in her decision-making?
3. How do you overcome doubt and build your confidence?
4. In the beginning of the book, did you think the wolf was "big and bad?" What did you think of the wolf by the end of the book?
5. Why do you think the author did not refer to the pigs as "little" and the wolf as "big and bad?"

6. Who was your favorite character and why?
7. Do you agree with Olivia's ruling? Do you believe it was fair? Why or why not?
8. Patrick and Penelope helped Paul bring his case against Walter. Who can you count on to have your back?
9. Act as Walter's lawyer. What other evidence could have helped Walter defend himself?
10. What do you think are the main points or themes of the story?

Wait, there's more!
Free Activities

Email
SugarCookieBooks@gmail.com
subject line
"3 Pigs Activities"
to receive extension activities like these, FREE!

**Stay Tuned
for the Next Chapter Book
in the Series featuring...**

GOLDILOCKS
&
THE 3 BEARS !!

E-mail
SugarCookieBooks@gmail.com
to subscribe for updates and special offers.

Sugar Cookie Books™

Andrew Learns about Lawyers

A wonderful children's book that will inspire the next generation of lawyers.

It's "Take Your Kid to Work Day" and Andrew is beyond excited to go to work with Mama until he realizes that he does not know what Mama does for work. "I am a lawyer or what some call an attorney," begins the exploration of the wonderful world of lawyers. By the end of each book, any child will be inspired to learn more about the career and the special pioneers of the field.

Visit the Sugar Cookie Books store
on www.teacherspayteachers.com
for book companion activities

Read Other Great Books by Tiffany Obeng

Career Books for Kids

Andrew Learns about Actors

Andrew Learns about Teachers

Andrew Learns about Chefs

Andrew Learns about Engineers

Andrew Learns about Scientists

Seasons Books for Kids

Winnie Loves Winter

Spencer Knows Spring

Fallon Favors Fall

Sonny Vibes Summer

SEL Books for Kids

Black Boy Hair Joy

My Summer Skin is Radiant

The Night The Lights Went Out

Two Houses Down

Scout's Honor

Sammy The Good Sport

Samantha the Good Sport

www.sugarcookiebooks.com

Made in the USA
Columbia, SC
12 October 2024